Arthur Weir

The Snowflake and Other Poems

Arthur Weir

The Snowflake and Other Poems

ISBN/EAN: 9783744720809

Printed in Europe, USA, Canada, Australia, Japan

Cover: Foto ©Andreas Hilbeck / pixelio.de

More available books at **www.hansebooks.com**

THE SNOWFLAKE

AND

OTHER POEMS

BY

ARTHUR WEIR

MONTREAL:

JOHN LOVELL & SON

1897

CONTENTS.

TO

HUGH GRAHAM, Esq.,

TO WHOSE

ENCOURAGEMENT, TASTE AND ENTERPRISE

THE AUTHOR

IS LARGELY INDEBTED

FOR

WHATEVER OF PUBLIC FAVOR HE ENJOYS,

THIS VOLUME

IS

Gratefully Dedicated.

ERRATA

Page 23, Second verse, first line, for "And" read "As."

Page 24, Second verse, last line, for "Thinkest" read "think'st."

Page 27, Third verse, third line, last word, read "athirst."

Page 86, Second verse, second line, for "a many" read "many a."

Page 44. for Conterbat. read "Conturbat" throughout.

THE SNOWFLAKE

AND OTHER POEMS.

THE SNOWFLAKE.

Fierce Neptune's daughter, beneath the water,
    In grottoes cool dwelt I,
And, laughing, hid in the seashell's lid,
    As fishes arrowed by.
My feet were free to the undersea;
    I played amidst its gloom,
And in the deep where the mermaids weep
    Above the hero's tomb,
Where the sea snake strips dainty maiden lips
    Of kisses once so warm,
And the lifeless child, by the eddies wild,
    Is torn from the mother's arm.
The foam-browed billow my head would pillow
    Upon its bosom fair,
While the restless sweep of the moon-led deep
    Would drift us here and there.
I oft would float in the dainty boat
    The Nautilus oared for me,
Out, far, far out, where a noisy rout
    Of breakers leapt in glee;
Or further urge to the world's dim verge,
    Where heaven meets the wave,
And the seagull's wing was the only thing
    To follow us was brave.

Then called by the blast, as it glided past,
      I would turn and clap my hands,
As the waves were tossed on the tropic coast,
      And furrowed the silver sands.

Where, with weedy locks, the bare limbed rocks
      Bend over the foaming sea,
I oft resorted, and, as I sported,
      The sunbeams played with me.
We would dance all day in the prismed spray,
      Or in the blossoms hide,
That, trembling, clung to the crags and hung
      Above the boiling tide.
Oftimes the cool, green depths of a pool
      Would lure me down to rest,
Till the sunbeams came in a path of flame
      And found me in my nest.
With colors gaily they decked me daily,
      And tempted me to fly
Afar from the foam of my ocean home
      Aloft in the cloudless sky.
But I said them nay, for the leaping spray,
      And cool, green depths of sea,
Than the flight of birds and the sunbeams' words
      Were dearer far to me.
"I had seen," I said, "to the sky o'erhead
      My sisters, laughing, soar
For a merry flight through the azure bright,
      And never saw them more.
I love my home in the ocean foam,
      I love the moonlit sands,

And I would sigh in the depths of sky
 And die in distant lands."

But who can prove to the plea of love,
 Unyielding and unkind ?
At love's low call we hasten all,
 Like leaves at the voice of wind.
And ere the moon at the night's high noon
 Had twelve times orbed grown,
My heart was stirred at a whispered word,
 My soul was not mine own.
My lover was fair as the balmy air
 That follows after storm,
When the careless sea, with a song of glee,
 Trips over the shallows warm.
He was the first through the gloom that burst
 To bring the dawn to me,
And he was the last from my sight that passed
 When darkness walked the sea.
One shimmering day, as asleep I lay
 Upon the tide-worn sand,
He stole apart, with an eager heart,
 From all the sunny band.
He came to me, as I lay thought free,
 And bent my couch above,
And while I slumbered, with words unnumbered,
 He pleaded for my love;
Then as I woke at the words he spoke,
 And rising turned to flee,
I was closely pressed to his ardent breast,
 And kisses were rained on me.

" My heart's own dearest," he cried, " why fearest
  Thou to take flight with me ?
Is there aught more fair than the realms of air
  In yonder sullen sea ?
Is the sea-gull's scream or the under gleam
  Of billows rushing by
More sweet to thee than the melody
  Of larks in the azure sky ?
Oh, be thou my bride, and side by side
  We'll float upon the breeze
O'er river and town, o'er forest and down,
  Wherever we twain shall please.
We'll swim in the wine of the luscious vine
  Which brims the crystal high,
And when of her lover the fond words move her,
  We'll dance in the maiden's eye.
We'll scale vast mountains and o'er gay fountains
  Hover in noon's warm glare,
And when night lowers, shall sleep in flowers
  That sway in the dewy air.
And shouldst thou tire, nor more desire
  The airy plains to roam,
But pine again for the leaping main
  And the drench of flying foam,
We need but glide on the leaf-sown tide
  Of some swift coursing stream
To our home at last, and the happy past
  Shall be but a varied dream."

I could but yield as he thus appealed,
  And clasping hand in hand,

With a parting glance at the sea's expanse,
    Dun rocks and silver strand,
We mounted high in the glowing sky,
    And, leaving home behind,
Fared swiftly forth to the distant north
    Upon the balmy wind.
O'er tangled brakes where the twilight makes
    For evermore its home,
And the tiger sleeps and the cobra creeps,
    And prowling jackals roam,
We floated fast, till the hills, at last,
    To bar our path appeared,
And many a peak its forehead bleak
    And tawny flanks upreared.
O'er many a cleft in the rocks bereft
    Of life and the sunlight's sheen,
Wild torrents were hurled to the under world,
    And wheeled the eagles keen.
In faltering lines, the famished pines
    Pressed up the mountain sides,
And sang to the blast, as it hurried past,
    The song of the ocean tides,
Till I yearned once more for the tropic shore
    Beside the emerald waves,
And my sisters gay and the dashing spray
    And ocean's weedy caves.

On, on we went, till the distance lent
    The hills an azure hue,
And the earth beneath was a naked heath
    Where winds in anger blew.

We saw the smoke like a wave that broke
    Above the homes of men,
And in the bowers of the meadow flowers
    Took rest for flight again.
A myriad sights were a thousand delights
    As on through space we sped,
But the happy day soon faded away
    And the sun in the west lay dead.
Then the shadows of death with their icy breath
    Drew ever more surely nigh,
And in frightened crowds the murky clouds
    Swept under the ebon sky.
Afar in the north a fire flamed forth
    And flickered with ghastly light,
Like a lamp that burns when a soul returns
    To God in the dead of night.
Gloom blotted the hills and the tinkling rills
    Were bound in frosty chains,
And the flowers once gay all lifeless lay
    Upon the dreary plains.
There was no sound in the air around,
    No voice upon earth below,
Save the angry beat of the wild winds' feet,
    That wandered to and fro.

In a frenzy of fear, with many a tear,
    I clung to my darling's breast,
For the wintry night with its baleful light
    My timorous soul distressed.
" Beloved," he cried, " sweet sea-nurtured bride,
    My love brings sorrow to thee,

For I feel at my heart the pitiless dart
    That Death has made keen for me."
I cried, " There are caves in the amethyst waves
    Wherein love may make life sweet,
Oh ! haste and return, ere the elements stern
    Have beaten us under their feet."
There was no reply to my passionate cry,
    No answering kiss to mine,
And I felt in the storm from my trembling form
    My lover's arms untwine.
All heavy he grew, like a wounded sea mew
    That dies in the midmost air,
And fell without sound to the frosty ground,
    And lay like a dead bird there.
The tresses of gold on his forehead cold
    I parted, and kissed his brow,
But his lips nor smiled at my fondling wild,
    His eyes nor knew me now.
And the icy blast, as it thundered past
    The hollow wherein he lay,
Tore him apart from my anguished heart,
    And carried him away.

I heard the trees moan in an undertone
    As the storm king struck them low,
And the river flood grew still as he stood
    And bade it cease to flow.
There was no flower in that sad hour
    Had strength to lift its head,
And I was alone in a land unknown
    And mourned my love for dead.

Then in countless hosts, like white-robed ghosts,
    My sisters lost drew near,
And hemmed me round, but they made no sound
    My breaking heart to cheer.
Each wore a star that glittered afar,
    Amid her flowing hair,
And they went and came like the lightless flame
    That pierced the northern air.
They floated high to the pitiless sky
    And gathered on the heath,
Till their myriad feet did mingle and meet,
    And hide the earth beneath.
And was it a dream that I should seem
    A snowy robe to don,
And tread without pleasure their swift, weird measure,
    As the wintry wind piped on.
Methought we flowed through that drear abode
    In sheets of spray and foam,
As erst with hope and mirth on the slope
    Of waves in our ocean home.

Then many a day in a trance I lay
    Upon the dreary plain,
Till, at last, I heard the pipe of a bird,
    And my heart grew warm again.
At the bird's sweet call through night's thick pall
    The faint sun peered and shone,
As of yore at home through the flying foam
    He looked from the gates of dawn.
He looked and smiled, and the air, beguiled,
    Grew warm and bright again,

And my sisters all each to each did call,
  As erst in the joyous main.
Like the leaping rills from the sunny hills
  That tinkle to the sea,
They sang as they glanced in the sun and danced
  On the rivers rushing free.
The flowers awoke from their sleep, and broke
  With many an emerald spear
And banner bright to the warm sunlight
  Through the leaves of the bygone year.
And one with a crown of gold bent down
  And took me to its heart,
" Poor waif of the storm," it said, " grow warm
  And share of my joy a part.
In the sky above there are many will love
  A heart as pure as thine;
Leave grief with the past, like the shadow we cast
  As we hasten where sunbeams shine."

I dwelt in the bower of the generous flower
  For many a quiet day,
Till, on soft winds blown, the seeds were sown ;
  And then I wandered away.
For sake of my love, the sun above
  Upraised me to the sky,
And east and west I went on my quest,
  But my dear one found not I.
Oft I heard from brooks in shadowy nooks
  My sisters call to me
To join their throng as they drifted along,
  Seeking the distant sea.

And hearing their lays in the woodland ways
    Through autumn's golden air,
A yearning came that I could not name,
    Stronger than my despair.
"If I must live on when my love is gone,"
    I murmured to my soul,
"Oh, let it be by the throbbing sea
    My sisters make their goal.
There let me rest like a child on the breast,
    Close to its great warm heart,
Till my sorrows cease and I am at peace,
    O lover, where thou art."
So I sought the brook, and the sky forsook,
    And reached the sea at last,
In whose briny waves and weedy caves
    I brood upon the past.

THE MASQUE OF THE YEAR.

(Time is discovered seated in the midst of a bevy of maidens, each of whom represents a month.)

TIME.

Behold me, Time, inexorable Time,
 Twin brother of Death. Like him all hearts I tame.
 As babes with baubles play, so I with fame.
I weigh all deeds, judge every poet's rhyme,
Sift heroes, smile at life's quaint pantomime,
 Put down the present great, and oft reclaim
 From sad oblivion some forgotten name,
Uplifting it to heights that are sublime.
I sit, amid the months, upon my throne,
 Waiting to greet the New Year drawing nigh,
And though it brings a destiny unknown,
 Naught need ye fear, since God is in the sky.
 Fate is God's choice ; be therefore of good cheer.
 Let mirth and song welcome each new crowned year.

JANUARY.

Far have I come, out of darkness, from chaos,
 The land of the future, dread realm unknown,
 Out of silence, alone.
I have trodden the ice-fields of drear Baccalaos,
 Heard the grinding of bergs in the seas of the
  north
 As the gale urged them forth,

And at midday have looked on the sun's feeble glory
  With a smile of disdain, for the warmth that he
    felt
  Ne'er my bosom could melt.
Death and stillness are mine, and, save wolves on a
    foray,
  All is still, all is shrouded, all Nature's asleep,
  Under snow hidden deep.
I am the ruler of uncreate chaos,
  Queen of absolute void, which life comes not
    anear—
  First month of the year.

FEBRUARY.

I am the month of beginnings. I bear
  In my bosom the seed of all changes to come.
  As yet I am dumb,
But Hope has been born in the breast of Despair.
  The pine boughs stir under their burden of snow,
  As though promise they know,
Yet the sun shines no stronger, there's naught that
    foretells
  The coming of summer. No song of a bird
  In the woodland is heard,
Not a sound, save the stroke of the axe, as it fells
  Some wood king, whose form sinks beneath the
    keen blade,
  With a crash, through the glade ;
Yet the spirit of Nature's awake, and the air
  Thrills with love. I soothe grief with my wonder-
    ful balm,
  Second month that I am.

MARCH.

I am the month of unrest and of yearning,
  Of wild and untamable hatred and love.
  I glide through the grove,
Calling on Summer, so slow in returning.
  I seek for the fruit, bud, leaf, blossom and all.
  When they heed not my call,
The winds I unleash, which, like hounds on the scent,
  Give voice round the farmsteads, and course o'er
      the moors,
  With a hundred detours,
Till they leap on the forests, whose branches are rent.
  I heap up the snowdrifts, bind firmer the streams,
  And defy the sun's beams.
My heart throbs with hate, and all tenderness spurn-
      ing,
  With winter again I span heaven's blue arch.
  I am passionate March.

APRIL.

I am the month of transition. My breast
  Heaves with sweet, delicate hope, that beguiles
  Dreamy Earth into smiles.
Through woodlands deserted I go on my quest,
  And summon the blood-root and shad-bush to
      flower
  Though they fade in an hour.
I drop gentle rain on the faded, brown grasses,
  And loosen the soil for all tender, green shoots,
  To push up from their roots.

I summon the birds, and where'er my foot passes,
  Sleeping Nature arouses itself at my call.
  I am helpful to all.
While no ecstacy's mine, I am never distressed,
  But tranquilly wander, to fate reconciled.
  I am April, the mild.

MAY.

I am the month of gay Summer's beginning,
  When earth with its verdure smiles up at the sky,
  And the mayflowers shy,
And sun-loving blossoms, their way to light winning
  Through strewn leaves of autumn, mute emblems
      of death,
  Perfume with their breath,
The zephyrs released from their fetters of frost.
  The streams murmur cheerily under their banks
  Their melodious thanks
For sweet freedom regained, as they flow and are lost
  In the broad, sunny river, that rushes along
  To the sea, with a song.
Chill Winter's forgot, with its woe and its sinning.
  Youth leaps in my veins—I am young, I am gay—
  I am love-kindling May.

JUNE.

I am the month of sweet, virginal joy,
  When Earth, as the sun its first passion discloses,
  Blushes with roses,
When all things are new, and nothing can cloy.
  The birds, in a cloudland of leafage concealed,
  By their songs are revealed.

All is young, all is love. In the shadowy vales,
    In woodland and meadow, all Nature's awake.
    At the wind's kiss, the lake
Breaks forth into smiles ; but as yet passion fails
    To weary itself. Soul is searching for soul,
    And has not reached its goal.
Life leaping to life doth each moment employ,
    And love doth all Nature's grand chorus attune.
    I am virginal June.

JULY.

I am the month of warm, passionate love,
    When Earth silent lies, with shy longings opprest,
    While soft sighs stir her breast.
All unclasped is her zone, and the Sun's warm lips
        prove
    Her lips ruby treasures, and make her soul his
    With many a kiss.
I wander abroad in the murmurous hours,
    While the silvery moonbeams sift down on the
        scene,
    Rustling leafage between.
I whisper of joy to the slumbering flowers,
    As, with petals close folded, like child hands in
        prayer,
    They rest on the air,
And I drop cooling dews from the clear sky above
    On the moist brow of Earth, as still she doth sigh.
    I am July.

AUGUST.

I am the month of sweet langour and dreaming.
 In the shadowy depths of the woods I recline,
 While afar stand the kine,
Thoughtful, knee-deep, where cool waters are stream-
    ing
 Over the sands, and at hand, loud and clear,
 The cicada I hear.
Afar, by the plunging green waves of the sea,
 I wander at times, when the shimmer of heat
 Disturbs my retreat;
Or amid rugged crags, where the wind wanders free,
 I sit in the shelter of hills, by the brook
 That leaps forth from its nook
Adown the swart cliff, with its silver spray gleaming,
 And I muse on the past with a rapturous sigh.
 Dreamy August am I.

SEPTEMBER.

I am the month that brings peace to the weary,
 The flush to the apple, the gold to the leaf,
 And the grain to the sheaf.
I am the month that prepares for the dreary,
 Long days of midwinter, when Earth lies asleep
 Under snow hidden deep.
After the yearning of Spring and the passion
 Of hot days of Summer, I cool the warm brow,
 And the seeds that the plough
Gave to earth I give back, shaped in daintier fashion.
 At the touch of my hand every toiler forgets
 All life's weeds and its frets,

And the heart that was grieving becomes again cheery.
    When I rule, men no longer their sorrows re-
      member.
    I am September.

OCTOBER.

I am the hush ere the coming of storm.
    I am the eventide, lulling to rest,
    Upon Earth's kindly breast,
Her offspring, the flowers, till they nestle up warm,
    Folding their leaves and their blossomy eyes
    Closing, child-wise.
I warn the still woodland, that doffs its gay dress
    And upsprings, like a warrior armed for the fray,
    To meet the dread day
When the Tempest's huge shoulders against it shall
      press.
    I breathe to the streams the fell tidings, until
    Every bickering rill,
With a tremor of fear, seaward hurls its lithe form
    In mad flight, ere with fetters the Ice King draws
      nigh.
    October am I.

NOVEMBER.

I am the priestess of frost, and I bring
    The winds in my train. I am vestured in snow,
    And wherever I go
The ice maidens deck me with jewels, and fling
    Crystal arches o'er streams that flow sombrely by
    Beneath the grey sky.

B

Earth under my feet a soft carpeting spreads,
    And from valley and hill, as I pass on my rounds,
    There re-echo no sounds.
The lean, famished forests bow down their high heads
    As among them I wander. The stars hold their
        breath
    As, dread omen of death,
Flits the mystic aurora with rustling wing
    High above, and some meteor falls like an ember.
    I am November.

DECEMBER.

I am the month when worn Earth lies at rest
    Under the eiderdown snow, that clings close
    To her form in repose,
As her gossamer drape to the virgin, whose breast
    Rises and falls as she dreams of her love.
    Through the keen air above
The stars glow like watch-fires of summer. Anon
    Come the jingle of sleigh-bells, a laugh and a shout,
    As gay youth, in mad rout,
Sweeps merrily down the white road, and is gone.
    Then silence returns, till the winds howl in glee,
    Or some frost-riven tree
Shrieks aloud in its pain. Yet Earth sleeps, undis-
        tressed.
    All ended her task, she has naught now to fear,
    December is here.

(The clock strikes)

January..	" One "	July...	.." Seven."
February.	" Two."	August..	" Eight."
March...	" Three."	September.. ..	" Nine."
April..	" Four."	October..	" Ten."
May..	" Five."	November.. ..	" Eleven."
June..	" Six."	December.. ..	" Twelve."

(The New Year Enters.)

THE NEW YEAR.

I am here, I have come from the home of the morning;
  I am flushed with hope's wine; I have treasures for
    all.
The old year is sped, let it serve as a warning
  That the moments I bring shall bear fruit ere they
    fall.
The past none can alter; its grief and its sinning
  Are writ for all time in the volume of life,
But behold me, the New Year, new records beginning ;
  Let love be their burden, not envy and strife.

CHORUS OF MONTHS.

Welcome, welcome, with chime of merry bell,
  Welcome to thy kingdom, O monarch pure and
    true !
In gladness we will serve thee. Ah ! rule this great
    earth well;
  Efface the sorrows of the past, and all past joys
    renew.
    We, the children of the sun,
    Who watch the precious moments run,

Will wreathe thy brow with stars of snow and flowers
  sweet and fair.
But while we sow the fruits of earth,
That man shall garner in with mirth,
To Time alone belongs the power
Of harvesting each ripened hour.
Welcome, welcome, with chime of merry bell !
  Another year is given to man to sow and reap his
  life.
When next the mystic book is sealed, what story will
  it tell ?
  Will it speak of love triumphant, will it tell of sin
  and strife ?
    O mortal man, remember
    Every year has its December,
And when the year has ended naught can change the
  record there.

THE MUSE AND THE PEN.

The Muse, renowned in ancient story,
  But seldom seen these humdrum times,
Came down to earth, in all her glory,
  To put new life in modern rhymes.
" Forsooth," she said, " I'm tired of hearing
  Mechanic singers, every one,
With forced conceits and thin veneering,
  Serving the lamp, and not the sun."

The Muse was but a simple maiden,
  Who loved the woodlands, meads and streams,
With odorous buds her gown was laden,
  Her hair was bright with rippling gleams;
And murmuring an Arcadian ditty,
  She wandered, with uncertain feet,
In wonder, through the crowded city,
  Bewildered by each clattering street.

She gazed upon the hurrying mortals,
  Each busy with his own affairs.
She spurned some lauded poets' portals,—
  " Let monthlies print such stuff as theirs."
A milkman nodded her a cheery
  " Bon jour, ma'mselle," in ready French,
And as she passed a cabman beery,
  He hiccoughed, " there's a likely wench."

She met a red-faced, buxom Chloe,
   A dapper Strephon, full of airs;
The one in vesture cheap and showy,
   The other versed in brutal stares;
And shocked and weary, hot and muddy,
   Into the nearest house she turned,
And found herself within the study
   Of one whose pen his living earned.

She looked quite curiously about her
   (Being of a curious turn of mind),
To learn if he did also flout her
   And still in life some pleasure find.
Shortly she marked his desk, half hidden
   Beneath a mass of copious notes,
And turned to it and read, unchidden,
   Of chartered banks and chartered boats.

She read that crops were thriving better,
   But that the country needed rain;
And then another item met her
   On "Watered stocks, the country's bane."
She read of "interest rates as under,
   With money still in poor demand,"
And let the item fall, to wonder
   Were poets wealthy in the land.

She read that "none who float on paper
   Long raise the wind, for all their craft,"
"Bulls up a tree, a market caper,"
   "A house in trouble with a draft."

She read of butter growing stronger
   And cheese more lively every day,
That baker's flour will rise no longer,
   And of "a serious cut in hay."

And still she turned the litter over,
   Reading an item now and then,
She did beneath the pile discover
   And pounce upon the writer's pen;
And by the charm the Muse possesses
   She made it speak like flesh and blood,—
Oh ! happy Pen, to have her tresses
   Fall round thee in that solitude !

" Dear Pen," she cried, " in what strange service
   Is this I find thy skill employed ?
Thy master's style seems bright and nervous,
   Yet is of sense a little void."
The Pen replied: " O gracious lady,
   Trade questions are considered here,
And thou wilt find transactions shady
   By master's hand made easily clear."

The pouting Muse her pretty shoulder
   Shrugged as she listened to the Pen.
" Thy master must than ice be colder
   If thus content to write for men.
Go, bid him frame a graceful sonnet,
   A simple poem from his heart,
And I will gently breathe upon it
   And to its body life impart."

Again the Pen: "O goddess puissant,
  My master lacks nor heart nor skill
To turn a stanza, but of recent
  Days he hath hungry mouths to fill.
He loves thee, but he may not show it,
  And Pegasus must drag the plough,
For men would starve him as a poet
  Who earns at least a pittance now."

The Muse waxed wroth: "Would not my beauty
  All else thy master make forget?"
The Pen replied: "The path of duty
  My master hath not swerved from yet.
Thy beauty haunts his every vision,
  Sweet on his ear thine accents fall;
Yet could he tread the fields Elysian,
  Thinkest thou, while suffering loved ones call?"

"But I can make his name immortal."
  "Immortal shame!" replied the Pen.
"When he should pass Death's sombre portal
  And stand before his God, what then?
He hath a God-like, awful function,
  To shield his own from want and wrong;
Wouldst have him, then, without compunction,
  Barter his birthright for a song?

"I am his trusted friend. Unflagging,
  I help him win his daily bread.
Though heart may ache, or thought be lagging,
  Still must the ink be ever shed.

Yet oft he lays me down, and, sighing,
　　Looks through the casement at the stars;
And then I know his soul is trying
　　Vainly to pass beyond its bars.

" A soldier in the war of labor,
　　He battles on, from day to day,
Swinging the gold-compelling sabre,
　　Nor finding time to pluck a spray.
Nay, more ! he must, through glorious bowers,
　　Press harshly on, with heavy tread,
Crushing to earth the beauteous flowers
　　With which he fain had wreathed thy head."

The Muse grew pensive.　Softly sighing,
　　She said: " Now pity him I can.
Strong, purposeful and self-denying,
　　Here I have what I seek, a Man.
Would that this noble self-surrender,
　　These high resolves, this purpose stern,
Might yet the grander verse engender,
　　And brighter make his genius burn !

" How grief must gnaw his heart asunder
　　As still Fate balks him, day by day ! "
" Nay ! " cried the Pen, " thou may'st wonder,
　　But know, my master's heart is gay.
Perchance at times, a pang concealing,
　　His face grows sad; but not for long,
For sweet, loved arms, around him stealing,
　　Fill all his soul with unvoiced song."

The Muse above the table bending,
  Laid her warm lips upon the Pen,
A thrill throughout its fibres sending:
  "This for thy master."   Slowly then,
She passed away; and after, never
  The writer labored, but a throng ·
Of fancies cheered him, singing ever:
  "The Muse hath crowned each unvoiced song."

THE BEAVER MEADOW.

'Tis a meadow green as an emerald's heart
  In the heart of an emerald wood,
And a crystal stream doth loiter and dart
  Through the sun-smitten solitude.
The orioles glance like flashes of fire
  From foliaged limb to limb,
And the harsh frogs pipe in a ceaseless choir
  From the marsh, when day grows dim.

When the grey, cold Dawn in her robes of mist,
  O'er meadow and wood and stream,
Looks forth from her tower of amethyst,
  She sees the wild duck gleam
In the slender reeds that have waded out,
  Far out, in the sinuous brook,
And she hears the loon, like a wary scout,
  Shrill keen from his secret nook.

Long years ago when our fathers first,
  Fearless and full of hope,
With love of venture and wealth athirst,
  O'er river and mountain slope,
To this woodland came, a lakelet lay
  As bright as a burnished shield,
Where now the rivulet waters play,
  And the loud frogs pipe, concealed.

And a wonderful town with its sunward domes,
  And wondrous people stood,
Where the deep mouthed frogs have now their homes,
  And the wild ducks lurk and brood.
Grand were the fronts and the pictured walls
  Of the Inca's ancient sway,
But the town that stood where the streamlet calls,
  More wondrous was than they.

Not a listless brain nor an idle hand
  Was there in all that town,
But strong defences the people planned,
  And hewed the great trees down.
The rippling stream, with consummate art,
  In barriers huge they pent,
And made their home in the new lake's heart,
  And dwelt therein content.

But woe to the town and its people all !
  Earth giveth no deathless joy,
And where man's merciless glances fall
  The simple they fain destroy.
The brutal and covetous Spanish horde
  That raided the Aztec land,
Put its people and chieftains to the sword,
  Its cities to the brand.

And here in this northern wilderness,
  This wonderful beaver town,
That baffled the elemental stress
  Before our sires went down.

Its stately domes and its barriers vast,
　Its sinuous streets, its lake,
The hunter destroyed and overcast,
　For a little riches' sake.

He slaughtered the noble beaver kings,
　And loosened the fettered stream.
And now the reeds, like a thousand strings,
　With music as of a dream,
In the night wind mourn the departed lake
　And the stately beaver town,
While the rippling waves in the rushes break,
　As the stream goes eddying down.

And musing here on the grassy site
　Of the beaver colony,
My soul is carried in fancy's flight
　To the site of Ville Marie,
Where the Hochelagans, or beaver race
　Of Indians, dwelt of old,
Their name renowned from their mountain's base
　To where the ocean rolled.,

Hochelaga the Beaver Meadow meant,
　And where the beaver dwelt
Long since, the white man pitched his tent,
　And before heaven knelt.
He felled the trees and he stayed the tide
　Of tribesmen rushing down,
And, like the beaver, he builded wide
　And strong a mighty town.

The curious skill and the council sage,
 And the beaver's love of toil,
Became as well his heritage
 As the broad and fruitful soil.
Then honor be to the beaver's name,
 And praise to the beaver's skill,
And in the labor that makes for fame
 May we all prove beavers still.

VOYAGEUR SONG.

Our mother is the good green earth,
    Our rest her bosom broad;
And sure, in plenty and in dearth,
    Of our six feet of sod,
We welcome Fate with careless mirth
    And dangerous paths have trod,
Holding our lives of little worth
    And fearing none but God.

Where, ankle deep, bright streamlets slide
    Above the fretted sand,
Our frail canoes, like shadows, glide
    Swift through the silent land;
Nor should, broad-shouldered, in some tide
    Rocks rise on every hand,
Our path will we confess denied,
    Nor cowardly seek the strand.

The foam may leap like frightened cloud
    That hears the tempest scream,
The waves may fold their whitened shroud
    Where ghastly ledges gleam;

With muscles strained and backs well bowed
    And poles that breaking seem,
We shoot the sault, whose torrent proud
    Itself our lord did deem.

The broad traverse is cold and deep,
    And treacherous smiles it hath,
And with its sickle of death doth reap,
    With woe for aftermath;
But though the wind-vext waves may leap,
    Like cougars, in our path,
Still forward on our way we keep,
    Nor heed their futile wrath.

Where glitter trackless wastes of snow
    Beneath the northern light,
On netted shoes we noiseless go,
    Nor heed though keen winds bite.
The shaggy bears our prowess know,
    The white fox fears our might,
And wolves, when warm our camp fires' glow,
    With angry snarls take flight.

Where forest fastnesses extend,
    Ne'er trod by'man before,
Where cries of loon and wild duck blend
    With some dark torrent's roar,
And timid deer, unawed, descend
    Along the lake's still shore,
We blaze the trees and onward wend
    To ravish nature's store.

Leve, leve and couche, at morn and eve
    These calls the echoes wake.
We rise and forward fare, nor grieve
    Though long portage we make,
Until the sky the sun gleams leave
    And shadows cowl the lake;
And then we rest and fancies weave
    For wife or sweetheart's sake.

DEDICATORY ODE.

*Read at the unveiling of the Monument erected in the Parliament Grounds
at Ottawa to the Memory of the Rt. Hon. Sir John A. Macdonald.*)

Here, in the solemn shadow of these walls,
  Wherein his voice long held the land in sway;
Here, where the cadence of the distant falls
  Seems a lament for grandeur passed away,
We, who have reaped where he had sown, now bring
  To him this thanksgiving,
This tribute to the unforgotten great,
  That, for all time, men may revere his name,
And children learn the secret of true fame,
  True greatness emulate.

We paid long since the tribute of our tears,
  When, at his post, the veteran statesman died ;
But now that grief has been assuaged by years,
  We mourn not, but rejoice, with sober pride,
That one of earth's immortals, wise and strong,
Dwelt in our midst so long,
  Teaching large thoughts and love of liberty,
And, Atlas-like, upon his shoulders bore
Our world of care, until, life's turmoil o'er,
  He passed from us away.

He found the seven sisters of the North,
  The Sea-Queen's daughters, in primeval woods,
By lonely streams, lamenting, and them forth
  He led from desert lands and solitudes.
The Pleiades of nations, they have shone
Upon Britannia's throne;
  With every passing year, their golden light
Waxing in lustre, until every land
In wonder looks upon the glorious band
  That breaks the Northern night.

He walked through life triumphant. Fortune's son,
  What were to others barriers, were to him
But gates, through which his high success was won.
  He held strange spirit commune with the dim
Shapes of the future. His far-reaching mind
Some harmony did find
  In elements discordant; and man's strength
And weakness served with him the noble end
To build a nation and all factions blend
  In brotherhood, at length.

And shall we, in whose midst so long he dwelt,
  Who had commune so long with his great mind,
Forsake his teachings, and, like Israel, melt
  Our gold to rear false gods ! Shall we grow blind
To those large thoughts, that tolerance which long
Made this Dominion strong ?
  Nay, never so ! He left an heritage
Worthy himself and us; be ours the pride
To bind this new Dominion, rich and wide
  Closer from age to age.

ENTERING PORT.

(In Memoriam The Rt. Hon. Sir John S. D. Thompson.)

Hark to the solemn gun and tolling bell !
  What ship is this, that, dark as night or death,
Is entering port upon the sullen swell,
  While an expectant nation holds its breath ?

From many a threatening port her cannon gape,
  Above her deck the flag of Britain flies;
Like some sad dream she comes, her sombre shape
  Crushing the waves that in her pathway rise.

One of the Sea Queen's ocean walls is she,
  Grim guardian of her honor, yet that prow
Ne'er upon nobler errand cleft the sea,
  Nor guarded Britain's honor more than now.

Day after day uprose the golden sun,
  Night after night it sank beneath the wave,
Pointing the vessel on that carried one
  The Empire honored to his western grave.

As Truth led that strong soul where'er it would
  Onward through strife to honor without stain,
So is he brought through ocean's solitude,
  With but the billows for his funeral train.

No warrior he the blood of men that shed,
   His was the higher task to make them one,
And Canada, awaiting now her dead,
   With tears attests the task was nobly done.

Yet, not within this sea-borne funeral car
   The patriot lies. He is no longer here,
But onward, upward still, he journeys far
   Beyond our ken to some still nobler sphere.

The harbor of his earthly wishes won,
   Fresh from new honors from his Sovereign's hand,
To him the summons came. Earth's voyage done,
   He set his bark towards the eternal strand.

He has gone forth, and leaves us but his name
   And this cold clay that waits the silent tomb;
Yet passing years shall never dim his fame,
   Nor love forget him in their gathering gloom.

With tolling bell and beat of muffled drum,
   With mournful boom of cannon, lay him down
Within the sepulchre, to which shall come
   Faintly the murmur of his native town.

In death he knit the Empire closer yet,
   Causing unnumbered hearts to throb as one.
Here by his tomb may Canada forget
   The bigotry that he had fain undone.

With his Queen's wreath upon his pulseless breast,
   Lulled by the murmur of the restless wave,
Life's voyage done, he takes his well-earned rest,
   In port, at last, with God beyond the grave.

WILD FLOWERS.

In Arcady, the happy swain,
　Who wandered through the woods and meadows,
Oft turned his head and oft was fain
　To start or smile at shifting shadows.
Sometimes, within a verdant brake,
　He saw a wood-nymph's graceful form
Gleam white, and felt her beauty make
　His heart beat fast, his cheek grow warm.

Sometimes while loitering by a brook,
　Whose ripples dreamy music made,
He spied in some sequestered nook
　A naiad, on the marge who played,
Or when the breeze the leafage stirred
　On drowsy summer afternoons,
Sometimes afar he thought he heard
　The satyrs pipe their merry tunes.

But Jupiter no longer wooes
　Antiope, nor Venus' lips
Tremble as she Adonis sues,
　And he from her embracement slips.
No longer nymph nor naiad now,
　Nor faun nor satyr haunts the wood,
Gone is Diana with her bow,—
　The woodland is a solitude.

Are nymph and naiad gone indeed,
  And is there now no Arcady ?
A fairy choir in wood and mead
  In gentle accents answer, " Nay."
And those who leave the world awhile
  With nature's spirit to commune,
May still see nymphs in woodland aisle
  And naiads bathe at sunny noon.

Beside the murmurous streams that wind
  Beneath the tangled foliage-meshes
Some sleeping naiad we may find,
  With charms the inmost soul deems precious.
And deep within the tawny shade
  Of pathless forests we may meet
Some true wood-nymph, who, unafraid,
  Receives us in her cool retreat.

At every step through sunny wood,
  Beneath our feet the wild flowers spring,
Nymphs of that sylvan solitude
  That us to love their beauty bring;   .
And still we follow, as of old
  The swain pursued the fleeting shape,
For once their graces we behold
  None can their mystic lure escape.

At every step beside the stream,
  Some nodding blossom beckons still.
We see its slender figure gleam
  Chastely beside the crystal rill.

Perchance it droops its dainty head,
  Or looks us fearless in the face,—
Ah, no, the naiads are not fled,
  The stream is still their dwelling-place.

Earth's turmoil has but dulled our ears,
  Its dust has but obscured our sight.
The pipes of Pan whoever hears
  Will see as well the woodland sprite.
The revels of the leaves and wind,
  The sudden glimpse of blossoming flowers,
These are his prize who leaves behind
  The world, and strays through Nature's bowers.

Oh, had I in Arcadia dwelt
  I would have watched for every gleam
Of shoulder, as some naiad svelt
  Clove the clear crystal of the stream;
I would have followed in pursuit
  Of artful nymph through tangled brakes,
And heard with joy the satyr's flute,
  Whose melody soft echo wakes.

And so, from earliest days of spring,
  When the first wild flower lifts its head,
Till autumn, when the breezes fling
  Broadcast the dying leaves and **dead,**
Through sensuous summer's golden hours
  I roam the vast Canadian woods,
Seeking the wild Canadian flowers,
  True nymphs of sylvan solitudes.

DEDICATORY BALLAD.

(*Written for the unveiling of the Monument erected by the Citizens of Montreal to Paul Chomedy de Maisonneuve.*)

The leaf in the forest had budded, of verdure a billowy
 sea
Over the woodland was flowing, o'erwhelming valley
 and lea.
The great river, bright in the sunshine, set the isle in a
 circlet of gold
As it swept to its tryst with the ocean, through realms
 of riches untold.

The slow-moving oar cleft the water, the balmy May
 breeze filled the sails,
As the wanderers drew near their haven, afar from the
 sea and its gales;
From the land of their fathers afar, and anear the keen
 Iroquois knives.
But the pilgrims, to fear ever strangers, to the Cross
 had entrusted their lives.

Not sordid were they.   Not the treasures of earth they
 had come to pursue,
Not for honor nor glory.   Far nobler the object our
 sires had in view.
To carry the cross to the savage, braving danger and
 hardship they came.
They came for the love of the Virgin, a city to found in
 her name.

Their hearts were o'erflowing with gladness. They,
    sang as they drew near the strand.
Their barks gently touched on the shingle, and Maison-
    neuve, leaping to land,
Bent his knee, and the others knelt with him, uplifting
    their voices in prayer
To the Ruler of all, while, prophetic, the priest in his
    vestments stood there.

The shadows of twilight were falling, the frog loudly,
    piped in the marsh,
The wild duck lurked in the shallows, and anear
    screamed the kingfisher harsh,
High above swept the night-hawk in circles, in the
    meadow the fireflies gleamed bright
And were caught, to adorn the rude altar with garlands
    of pulsating light.

The wanderers calmly sought slumber. The sentinel
    stood at his ease,
The rivulet gurgled and eddied, and answered the mur-
    muring trees,
The mountain loomed dark in the distance, and the
    wolf looking down from the height,
In wonder and awe, saw the camp fire that burned on
    a city's birth night.

If you ask how that mustard seed flourished, and spread
    its great branches abroad,
If you ask at what sacrifice nourished or watered with
    what noble blood ?

Lo ! the pages of history answer.   There 'tis written
    in letters of gold
How each was a Christian and soldier, who founded
    Ville Marie of old.

They lived on the confines of chaos.   Whenever the
    savage horde broke
On the ill-fated colony, they were the first whose arm
    parried the stroke.
They were Dollards in heart, and went even to torture
    and death with a smile,
While the women, like angels of mercy, stanched their
    wounds and their woes did beguile.

None braver, and no one more gentle, none wiser in
    council than he,
Maisonneuve, this, the new world's defender, who for
    God held his whole life in fee.
He led them in worship, consoled them when thickly
    their troubles did fall,
Maisonneuve the undaunted, the founder, Æneas of
    old Montreal.

And here where he battled lone-handed with savages
    thirsting for blood,
Where now beats the pulse of a city, the heart of a new
    nationhood,
Long years may his monument stand that our children
    may ask and be told
Of the leader who founded Ville Marie, and honor the
    heroes of old.

TIMOR MORTIS CONTERBAT ME.

(The Fear of Death Affrights Me.)

Shall I too sing, as he sang of old,
  The tuneful singer beyond the sea,
When life's flame sank and his blood waxed cold,
  Timor mortis conterbat me.

Earth is so fair to look upon,
  And life so sweet, though there sorrows be,
Why welcome the summons to be gone ?
  Timor mortis conterbat me.

Wife that I love as the sea the moon,
  Babes that prattle about my knee;
Has heaven itself a dearer boon ?
  Timor mortis conterbat me.

Is there heaven at all or only the grave
  With the lisp of rain in the willow tree,
Will the after death give all I crave ?
  Timor mortis conterbat me.

Will there be ideals still to follow,
  And truths, like nymphs my pursuit to flee,
Or will the ancient faith prove hollow ?
  Timor mortis conterbat me.

Are there golden suns in a golden noon,
   Are there grey, still dawns on a dewy lea,
Are there twilights there, with a crescent moon ?
   Timor mortis conterbat me.

Are there aims to spur me and goals to reach,
   Are there wondrous lands for the eye to see,
Is melody there and dulcet speech ?
   Timor mortis conterbat me.

Does friend meet friend and love meet love,
   Greet and converse with sober glee,
Or is all new in the courts above ?
   Timor mortis conterbat me.

Is heaven like earth on a nobler plan,
   As in dreams we image it, hopefully,
Or does the Spirit forget the Man ?
   Timor mortis conterbat me.

Shall I be I when the death-throe's past,
   Soul from the flesh set only free,
Or in new mould shall I be recast ?
   Timor mortis conterbat me.

If heaven be not akin to earth,
   I shall not be I, if I happy be.
If I be not I, what is heaven worth ?
   Timor mortis conterbat me.

ON NEW YEAR'S EVE.

The wintry moon was streaming
   Through the window, silvery-clear,
And I sat in my study, dreaming
   Sweet dreams of the coming year.

There was no sound save the laughter
   Of flames on the gusty hearth,
As hour followed fleet hour after
   To welcome the Year with mirth.

Then, sharp through the solemn quiet,
   I heard in the gloomy hall
The scamper of mice run riot,
   And I heard them in the wall.

I leaned on my hand and listened
   To hear the cravens go,
While paler the moonbeams glistened
   And the fire on the hearth burned low.

And was I awake, or sleeping,
   That, close by the door, I heard
The voice of a woman weeping
   The sigh of a farewell word?

And was it the night wind mocking
   That tapped and opened the door,
Or was it a woman knocking
   And a light step on the floor?

I saw at my side a maiden
   With tears in her gentle eyes,
And her shapely arms were laden
   With gems from time's argosies.

On her brow was a white star shining,
   On her breast was a lily fair ;
But of rue was a sad wreath twining
   Among her golden hair.

From my chair to her dear side springing,
   I greeted her with a kiss,
For I thought her the New Year, bringing
   New uncut jewels of bliss.

She blushed at my warm embraces
   And joy in her sweet face shone,
As sunlight a shadow chases
   While a summer cloud floats on.

I said : " I have long been yearning,
   New Year, to behold thy face."
Pale grew the maid, and, turning,
   She shrank from my close embrace,

And wept : " Oh ! thou fickle hearted
   The depth of my love to prove,
Yet ere from my bosom parted
   To sigh for an untried love.

' I brought thee the rarest treasures
   Time's treasury could bestow ;
I sated thy days with pleasures,
   And guarded thy heart from woe.

" Thy wish I refused thee never.
   I granted thee love and peace ;
Yet thou scornest me now, or ever
   My labor for thee doth cease.

" See, here are the gifts I showered
   Thy life's pathway upon,
And now that thou hast been dowered
   With all, canst thou wish me gone ?

" O thankless heart, wilt thou never
   Be satisfied with thy lot,
Or must thou be pining ever
   For joys that as yet are not ?

" And turn from my fond embraces
   An utter unknown to greet,
As a child a butterfly chases
   Treading flowers beneath his feet ? "

Then, like the great sun springing
   Through night to a tropic dawn,
My heart, to the Old Year clinging,
   Yearned for the joys nigh gone.

And oh, what a wave of sorrow
   Passed over my grieving soul,
As I thought of the new to-morrow
   That led to some unknown goal!

" Oh, stay," I cried, soul-shaken,
   " Heed not the flight of time,
Oh stay,"—But I was forsaken,
   And heard the New Year chime.

IN THE CLOSING HOURS.

In the closing hours of night,
    When the latest guest has gone,
By the hearth fire's flickering light
    Sweet it is to dream alone.

Sweet the social joy, and sweet
    Strife that ends in victory;
Sweeter still the peace complete
    Following on the eager day.

Then how sweet the lassitude,
    Revelling in romantic rest,
Buoyed on dreams, whose mystic flood
    Draws the soul on happy quest.

In the closing hours of life,
    When the friends of youth are gone,
Ended lust of gain and strife,
    Peace approaches with the dawn.

Sweet the rest and solitude
    When the hair is turning white,
While the past, with broadening flood,
    Murmurs through the closing night.

WHERE HEAVEN IS.

When the babe is swung in its pearly cot, the warm sun ·
        shining, the song-birds gay,
Cool shades among, in its lacework grot, the child
        reclining doth dreamful sway.
Hope's hand, entwining life's harp new strung with
        joyous garlands, its sound doth stay,
And he thinks earth heaven, to him God-given, nor cares ·
        though the passing hours delay.

From the threshold of life on the bright pathway that⁻
        stretches afar to the infinite,
Youth yearns for the strife, as a child for play, and his
        dreamings are of a well-won height.
As at dawn of day when the Morning Star unbinds the ·
        zone of the virgin Light,
We watch, all breathless, for beauty deathless, so heaven's
        beyond us, yet seems in sight.

And then, ah, then, as the years go by, and hope grows
        weary with waiting long,
When trust in men we must fain deny, the *miserere*
        replaces song.

Like slaves that ply in the galley's den the laboring oar,
    through sin and wrong,
The soul plods on, and heaven is gone; we can but suffer
    and yet be strong.

When the snows of age fall thick and fast, and passion
    has faded like flowers that grow,   ·
The memory sage dreams dreams of the past and all
    that has made it have joys below.
When the friends long laid in the grave, at last, stand
    beckoning us in the twilight glow,
And wrongs endured prove that which cured, the heaven
    behind us too late we know.

The heaven of man is never here; it always is where his
    treasures are.
To-day's brief span arches little dear; the stream of bliss
    seems wider afar.
From this to this the path is drear; there's always some-
    thing each joy to mar,
Till the past that is real becomes ideal under the gold
    of life's twilight star.

NEW YEAR'S EVE.

Air—Belle Mahone.

Hark! the tolling of the bells.
How it sinks and how it swells!
O'er the sleeping town it knells,
  " *Fare thee well, Old Year.*"
Far across the snowy plain
Rolls the many-tongued refrain,
And the echoes cry again,
  " *Fare thee well, Old Year.*"

Thou hast been a kindly year,
Thou hast spared us many a tear,
Thou hast vanquished many a fear,
  Fare thee well, Old Year.
Lightly touched by summer showers,
Budding hopes have grown to flowers,
Happy days have flown like hours,
  Fare thee well, Old Year.

Many a lesson thou hast taught,
Precious favors thou hast brought,
Pleasant changes thou hast wrought,
  Fare thee well, Old Year.

Now thy rule is near an end,
Thy last records have been penned,
We must part at last, true friend.
    Fare thee well, Old Year.

Close and seal the book of fate,
With whate'er it may relate,
Sin and goodness, love and hate,
    Fare thee well, Old Year.
One more volume is complete,
Take it to the Mercy Seat,
Lay it at the Master's feet,
    Fare thee well, Old Year.

REFRAIN.

Fare thee well, Old Year,
Fare thee well, Old Year,
Thou hast been a faithful friend,
Fare thee well, Old Year.

PEGASUS.

If you find Pegasus a steed
   Scornful of your control,
Who canters well enough, indeed,
   But will not caracole,
So much the better, poet mine,
   'Tis bottom wins the race.
Let poetasters prance, in fine ;
   Keep you the steady pace.

Let poetasters hunt for sound,
   Chase metres, out of breath ;
Great thoughts are not thus run to ground,
   Nor fame in at the death.
So, let your Pegasus be free
   To hunt some thought sublime,
While you sit still, with clinging knee,
   And gallop simple rhyme.

Ah, friend, of all the joys of earth,
   There's nothing like the hunt,
The good horse straining at the girth,
   The clear-tongued hounds in front.

And if your Pegasus can bear
   You well before the rout,
Don't curb and make him beat the air;
   Loose rein, and let him out.

Oft when a poet's rhymes I read,
   With ornate language wrought,
Its cadences, though sweet indeed,
   But hide the lack of thought.
Be yours the poem that can stand
   From trappings wholly free,
Each thought a Phryne, to be scanned
   In fearless nudity.

IT WOULD BE EASY TO BE GOOD.

Who walks the paths of righteousness
    Or follows ways of evil,
Who knows the joys that angels bless
    Or sin's insensate revel,
At last, too well has understood
    Sin is not worth a feather.—
It would be easy to be good,
    If all were good together.

Waiving the conscience we offend,
    And weighing but the pleasure,
Though we all sinful joys might blend,
    They make a sorry treasure.
The loftiest joys must be subdued,
    The soul we fain must tether.—
It would be easy to be good
    If all were good together.

Oh, would that man might give free scope
    To every gentle feeling !
The soul would realize its hope
    Its noblest side revealing.

Would man might trust man's brotherhood
  In calm and stormy weather.—
It would be easy to be good
  If all were good together.

If no one schemed to do a wrong,
  No need for wrong were given ;
If each his neighbor helped along,
  This earth would be a heaven ;
If men once met in rectitude,
  Farewell, the regions nether.—
It would be easy to be good,
  If all were good together.

THE LITTLE TROOPER.

Swift troopers twain ride side by side
　　Throughout life's long campaign.
They make a jest of all man's pride,
And oh, the havoc!　As they ride,
　　They cannot count their slain.

The one is young and debonair,
　　And laughing swings his blade.
The zephyrs toss his golden hair,
His eyes are blue ; he is so fair
　　He seems a masking maid.

The other is a warrior grim,
　　Dark as a midnight storm.
There is no man can cope with him.
We shrink and tremble in each limb
　　Before his awful form.

Yet though men fear the sombre foe
　　More than the gold-tressed youth,
The boy with every careless blow
More than the trooper grim lays low,
　　And causes earth more ruth.

Keener his mocking sword doth prove
  Than flame or winter's breath.
Men bear his wounds to the realm above,
For the little trooper's name is Love,
  His comrade's only Death.

CUPID'S DISGUISES.

Dan Cupid wears disguises.
  We never see his form,
Till suddenly he surprises
  And takes the heart by storm.

He hides at times in the blushes
  That tinge a cheek so fair,
Or oft in the moonlit hushes
  In a sweet voice on the air.

Sometimes he's in the dancing
  Of mirth in azure eyes,
Sometimes in the curve entrancing
  Of lips that part in sighs.

And sometimes in the glimmer
  Of arm, rich lace beneath ;
Sometimes in the tresses' shimmer,
  Sometimes in the peep of teeth.

Oh, he's a little bandit,
  And bold as bold can be.
He leads us, single-handed,
  Into captivity.

For none is a match for Cupid.
He swifter is than thought.
The keenest mind is but stupid,
When he begins to plot.

.

MUSIC.

Life hath such longings, bitter sweet,
   And yet so few it satisfies
That man fain dreams life is complete
   Only beyond the skies.

And like the mystic cloud of fire
   That guided Israel's way by night,
Every unsatisfied desire
   Leads man towards the right.

Around him, mingling with the dust,
   Youth's pure ideals, shattered, lie ;
Hope, virtue, charity and trust
   Amid life's deserts die.

Fade aspirations, fades each dream
   Of goodness, honor and renown.
Man floats on a polluted stream,
   Which fain would drag him down.

But music, like the nightingale
   That sweetly sings in woodland brakes,.
When hope and trust and virtue fail,
   Man's nobler nature wakes.

Only in music doth man find
　　An echo of the dreams of youth,
When he saw gods among mankind,
　　In woman only truth.

BABY'S STOCKING.

Baby's dainty little stocking
   Hangs beside his wicker cot,
Darling mother's wishes mocking
   And the treasures she has brought.

For it is so small that never
   Gift can find a place inside.
Was there doting mother ever
   So distressed at Christmas tide?

Baby's eyes are closed and dreaming
   Of the gentle mother face;
Baby's hands are clasped and seeming
   Interlocked in fond embrace.

Baby's lips are softly smiling,
   And the Rubicon of youth
He has passed, for lo! beguiling
   Mother's kisses, peeps a tooth.

Naught for gifts is baby caring.
   Santa Claus has many a gem,
But, God's love and mother's sharing,
   Baby has no need of them.

E

MY DIVINITY.

I am a god ; yes, I,—
  (Smile, if you will, at the claim)
Mote though I am in the ambient sky,
  Housed, I confess, in putrescible frame,
Still, a divinity.

My sceptre I claim, and, perchance,
  My altars as well,—who knows ?
You would prick my pride with your wit's keen
      lance,
  You know my radius. Well, suppose
You pipe, I dance.

Am I the Primary Cause ?
  That's my affair, not my creatures'.
Did I create nature's adamant laws,
  Or am I but one of her manifold features ?
Fellow gods can pick flaws !

But the little corpuscles of blood
  I create by millions each hour,
Do you fancy the witless ephemeral brood,
  As each lives its life, can my limits and power
Declare understood ?

Alone in the grey of my brain
   I sit and my universe rule.
What can they know of their god, though they fain
   Question, perhaps, each contemptible fool,
What joy is, why pain ?

Do they brag of their universe, boast,
   Worsting some hostile bacillus,
Fight over their God, sect term other sect lost,
   Read my ways or complain, " Why torment us
      and kill us ? "
What fate has each ghost ?

Perfecting some large thought that may
   Move the earth that I dwell on,
A million my creatures, remorseless, I slay.
   Am I annoyed if they call me a felon !
It is I, or they.

My work, for their sake, shall I cease,
   My very nature disjoint ?
Is there aught but destruction for all in such peace ?
   Must I miracle work for a microscope point,—
Corpuscles to please ?

We are not one, we are twain,
   Yet are we one and not two.
They are the universe, I am the brain,
   In and about them, knit through and through,—
Chords in one strain.

In common we have, at least, this,
  Creator and creature, that we
Must rise to the height of our powers, or miss
  Life's best for ourselves, and each other decree
Frustrate of bliss.

.   .   .   .   .   .

Is, now, this godhead of mine,
  My limits, this difference vast
Between creature and maker, a symbol? In fine
  Is mankind but a host of blood corpuscles, massed
Through the Divine?

THE SLEEPING SOUL.

Will ever thy soul awake,
Awake and come smiling to greet my own?
Will ever the love-light break
From thine eyes upon me, like the sun
On the billows that shoreward run,
Into foam by the winds of the ocean blown?

To me seems thy pure soul sleeping.
Thou hast in thy heart a bird,
But its head is under its wing.
I watch it and think with weeping
How sweet a song it might sing ;
Yet by love it is never stirred.

Oft in the hush of a drowsy night
I dream that I hear that low bird voice
Lilting so merrily,
Singing so cheerily,
Bidding my heart to its depths rejoice ;
But alas, takes flight
My dream before the dawn's lance of light.

Alas, it is not for me
To kiss thy soul, as the prince in story
Kissed the Sleeping Beauty's lips,
And to a life-love waken thee.
Round thee there is a maiden glory
Fairer than circles the sun that dips
Into the sea while chill night comes creeping
Slowly, silently through the sky;
But as well might I
Reach out my hand to the sun and try
To make his glory my very own
As think to touch with my finger tips
Thy glorious beauty that shrinks from me.

THE MOTHER.

Down the bright pathway of life, where joy, like the
throstle, was singing,
She passed, like a sungleam at dawn, through mist-
lands of sorrows and fears,
Seeking the soul of the babe at her bosom now nursing
and clinging,
And stood in the valley of death, gloomed with the
shadow of tears.

Ghost glided past after ghost, and shook ghastly arms
at the mortal
Who dared to the valley of pain go down for the winning of life.
Hour after hour trembled by, as we crouched in our woe
at the portal,
Made strangers to her whom we loved by strangers
who looked on her strife.

Angels spake hope to her there, as she stood in the vale
of the shadow,
Demons snarled at her heels, she was haunted by
visions abhorred ;

But Love was a lamp to her feet as she passed through
    the woe-blossomed meadow,
  Seeking the soul of her child. She was brave, for her
    trust was the Lord.

Death turned his sword as she came, and she passed
    through the gateways of heaven,
  Treading the pavements of pearl and haloed with
    shimmering gleams,
On, till the veil hung between immortal and mortal was
    riven,
  And she brought from the garden of God the blue-
    eyed flower of her dreams.

PLUCK FLOWERS IN YOUTH.

Pluck flowers in youth, nor heed how old tongues prate ;
Pluck flowers in youth, in age it is too late ;
   Pluck flowers when it is morn with flowers and you.
So soon they wither, do not hesitate,
   Lest you should gather roses not, but rue.
Pluck flowers ere life grows cold and desolate,
       And love turns hate.

Pluck flowers in youth ; age is the time for wheat ;
To age not even the rose itself is sweet,
   Pluck flowers,pluck flowers in youth,while faith is great,
Ere life and joy grow cankered with deceit.
   Pluck flowers in youth ; no sadder thought brings Fate
Than memory of scorned joys crushed by our feet
       In flight too fleet.

O FOOLISH HEART.

O foolish heart, to flutter so
   With hope and fear;
O treacherous blush, to come and go
   When he is near;
Why do ye to the world reveal
The passion I would fain conceal?

O ears, that love to hear him speak;
   O downcast eyes,
Whose lashes droop upon each cheek,
   Nor dare to rise;
Do ye not know she sees and hears
Fond looks and words that cost me tears?

Be brave, mine heart, if he despise,
   Give scorn for scorn;
Be deaf, mine ears, be blind, mine eyes,—
   Yet soul, why mourn?
Though she may claim him for her own,
My love, my love is mine alone.

MY HEART'S A MERRY ROVER.

My heart's a merry rover,
   Though innocent of wrong ;
Forever beauty's lover,
   Yet never constant long.

When coral lips are pouting,
   Their smiling to disguise,
He kneels and loves, not doubting
   They are his richest prize.

Yet when, amid his dreaming,
   He spies a bosom fair,
At once the rogue is scheming
   To gain admittance there ;

Though should he see the tresses
   That frame a pretty head,
His love and his caresses
   He spends on them instead.

Then, if bright eyes confuse him
   With many a saucy stare,
The lips, the curls, the bosom
   Must mourn their worshipper.

And yet this merry rover
  Is nothing if not true,
He's but one maiden's lover,
  And, dearest, she is you.

THE CIGARETTE SMOKER.

Mark her as she stands,
  Blue eyes bright, match alight,
Shielding with her hands
  The growing flame,
Holding to her lips, where the bee, love, sips,
The fragrant pleasure of man's leisure,
  Cigarette by name.

There! it makes her cough.
  If she smoke, must she choke
When blue whirls come off?
  Now she denies
The cigarette the bliss of her lips' sweet kiss,
Holds it burning, to ash turning,
  Till at last it dies.

Thus she lit my heart,
  By the fell magic spell
Of love's witching art,
  And just as I
Burned with passion's fire, shrank from my desire,
Let my yearning and heart-burning
  Into ashes die.

TAKE ME AS YOU FIND ME.

Take me as you find me,
 Take me so,
Else from love unbind me,
 Let me go.

Two twin gifts God gave me,
 Body and soul ;
These shall lose or save me,
 As years roll.

I can never alter ;
 I must wend
Onward, thus, nor falter
 To the end.

If you love, then, love me,
 Sweetheart, so
You'll not look above me,
 Nor below.

AT THE TRYST.

The evening stars are shining
　Amid the gloom of air,
Like gold and jewels twining
　Among thy golden hair.

They guard the dawn's shut portal
　And count the moments fleet,—
O maiden, we are mortal,
　Why hasten not thy feet?

The moonlight and the shadows
　Are wooing by the stream,
And far across the meadows
　Thy windows brightly gleam.

My eager heart is beating
　Beneath the trysting tree,
The evening hours are fleeting,
　Why com'st thou not to me?

SONNETS IN CALIFORNIA.

ON A FLASK OF WATER.

Taken from the Pacific at Santa Monica, Cal.

From seas Alaskan, where, through sunless days,
  The grinding ice floes cast a spectral glare,
  I come to shores where, through the golden air,
Palms wave and bees dip in the orange sprays.
From shores Siberian, where the keen knout preys
  On women, wan with torture and despair,
  I come, a voiceless, palpitating prayer,
Where Freedom dwells, yet succor still delays.

From far Cathay, the oldest land of lands,
  A giant sunk in poppied, dreamful rest,
I come where earth's great last-born nation stands,
  Flower of the centuries, the titanic West.
I come where East and West stand face to face,
The childhood and the manhood of the race.

SPRING IN THE SOUTH.

Through the quaint southern winter without snow,
  Without an icy blast or chilling air,
  When the broad mesas arid lie and bare,
The Ishmael cactus and the sage brush grow.

The golden orange bends the lithe branch low,
　The sunflowers throng the by-ways everywhere,
　Palms wave, birds sing.　The earth lies free of care,
Basking in skies one golden, cloudless glow.

Then come the rains, and in their cortege bring
　Streams to the canyons, and to ranch and glen
　　Wild flowers and orange blossoms, wherein rides
The bee on golden zephyrs.　Swiftly then,
　Like wind-blown fire, up the Sierra sides
A blaze of poppies runs, and it is Spring.

A WINTER DAY.

In the Sierras.

O'er the Sierras scarce the moon yestre'en
　Was risen to flood each sombre peak with light,
　Ere came a cloud host through the gusty night,
Storming the crags.　Sheer canyon walls between
They swept, and hid bare ledge and living green.
　Hoarse thunder pealed from unseen height to height,
　As though the vast hills boasted of their might,
Though Chaos' self upon them seemed to lean.

Dawn drew aside night's veil of mist, and came
　Across the hills.　The clouds retired, and lo!
　　On every wind-swept crag, as Day looked forth,
Bright in the southern sunshine gleamed the snow,
　　A vision of the unforgotten North
'Twixt golden skies and poppy fields aflame.

F

In the Valley.

Snow on the hills, but in the valley, flowers,
  Poppies aflame and orange blooms, whose scent
  With the faint odor of the snow is blent.
Snow on the peaks, but in the canyons, showers,
And torrents drinking strength from stormy hours.
  The geese wheel seaward through the clouds half spent,
  Fleeing the snow and screaming discontent,
But in the vale birds trill in blossomy bowers.

Summer is in the vale, though in the heights
  The bandit Winter lurks to seize his prey.
    Still springs the grain, vines grow and fruit delights
  Sun and soft winds through many a golden day
    In many an Eden valley, nestling warm
Below the stern Sierras, wrapped in storm.

THE POOL OF SANT' OLINE.

Sierra Madre, Cal.

Ere yet the Spanish cavalier
   For this new world set sail,
Ere yet the padres came anear
   San Gabriel's sunny vale,
Ere yet the thirst for gold drew men
   Across the western hills,
I rippled down this rocky glen,
   The happiest of rills.

The shadows of the spreading oak
   Oft lay upon my breast ;
Oft through the brown madronas broke
   The bear upon his quest.
Past starry yuccas, to my brink,
   At many a crimson dawn,
The mountain lion came to drink,
   And oft a timid fawn.

The golden moments came and went
   Of many a sunny year,
And still I rippled on, content
   And solitary here.

At times a weary miner came
  And quaffed my cooling stream,
At times I saw the camp-fire flame
  Of hardy hunters gleam.

Though oft I paused to hear some bird
  Trill in the leaves above,
A maid I never saw nor heard,
  Nor knew the name of love.
Oh, there was never rivulet
  So merry in a glen ;
But now I never can forget,
  Nor merry be again.

She came, in thoughtless, girlish mood,
  The dizzy trail along.
Upon my ferny marge she stood
  And listened to my song.
I saw her, and I leapt for glee
  In many a lucent wave,
And when she stooped to drink from me,
  My very heart I gave.

She passed, and now no more I sing
  Among the granite hills ;
Instead, my ceaseless murmuring
  The sombre canyon fills.
Oh! ye to whom that maid divine
  Hath also heartless been,
Come join your mournful plaint with mine,
  The pool of Sant' Oline.

WINTER IN THE SOUTH.

At home the blossoms are asleep
  Beside the frost-bound rills ;
At home the snow is drifting deep
  Upon the windy hills ;
At home the ice king mocks the sun,
  The woods are drear and bare,
And of the birds there is not one
  Left singing anywhere.

But here the fields are green with grain,
  The mesas bright with flowers.
The birds repeat each dulcet strain
  They learned in Eden's bowers.
'Midst ripening fruit, the orange trees
  Have mingled odorous blooms,
And here and there the eager bees
  Hum through the golden glooms.

The swart Sierras, crowned with snow,
  Stand knee deep in the green,
Like patriarchs smiling as they go
  Blithe groups of youth between.

Behind them is the burning sand
  Of the Mojave* waste ;
Before, the warm Pacific strand,
  By golden seas embraced.

When in the palm tree's shade I rest
  Through a many perfect day,
My heart would fain forget life's quest,
  And live in dreams alway ;
But when upon the snow-clad hills
  Mine eyes again look forth,
I wake.   Thy spell my bosom thrills,
  Stern homeland in the north !

Give me the seasons of the year,
  The bursting of the leaf,
The northern summer brief but dear,
  And autumn's golden sheaf.
Give me the wintry moon's pale gleam,
  With snow and storm at strife.
The south is a bewitching dream,
  But in the north is life.

---

* Pronounced Mohavy.

THE KINDERGARTEN.

O blossoming lives that to the fruits
   Now ripened for the gathering in,
Speak of old days, ere life's pursuits
   Touched the new soul with taint of sin,

We who now watch you at your game,
   We, weary of the toil and strife,
Must envy you your scorn of fame,
   Your eager, loving trust in life.

Perchance, the babe that, thoughtless, piles
   His blocks unsteadily in air,
May yet a minster build, whose aisles
   Shall echo to a nation's prayer.

Perchance, the child that scarce can tell
   The letters on his cubes of wood,
May yet with a poetic spell
   Charm and uplift the multitude.

They question not, they only live
   To pluck the blossoms of each hour.
Ambition frets them not, they give
   No thought to pomp or place or power.

We too have toys, and we pursue
  Our trivial aims ; we rage and sigh
Because our blocks are built askew,
  And our best hopes in ruins lie.

Yet over us, as over these,
  A teacher watches, true and kind,
Striving to guide our fantasies,
  And patient with the groping mind.

From flower of wisdom unto flower
  He leads us, as these babes are led,
Till chimes, at last, the closing hour,
  The prizes won, the lessons said.

And happy he who in this school
  Of life, that fits the soul for death,
Has learned to serve as well as rule,
  And speak for truth with every breath.

THE POET.

The budding flower that wakes at dewy morn
 Attains perfection through the sun-swept day,
And poets, to life's highest mission born,
 By slow unfolding reach the perfect lay.

And like the harp, attuned to every breeze,
 That in the open casement sighs or sings,
The poet soul is void of melodies
 Till unseen spirit fingers sweep the strings.

Life, the magician, with his subtle powers,
 Death, the dark helmsman over seas unknown,
Nature, all-mother, and the teaching hours
 Through him their grand, mysterious chants intone.

And oft his numbers falter, and his song
 In discord breaks, ere he can hymn again
The anthems of the wondrous spirit throng,
 And voice strange thoughts beyond our mortal ken.

And oft the world and the world's sins immesh
 His soul, which still the pitying spirits calm ;
And in the warfare between soul and flesh
 His heart oft rises to the noblest psalm.

But should he cease to wage the upward strife,
   Or thrall himself a slave to evil's power,
Too proud the Muse to bless a craven life,
   Too pure, a sinful heart with song to dower.

For the true poet, throwing down his gage
   To fate, fights upwards far beyond life's mist,
And with the broadened vision of the sage
   Beholds all earth by hope's warm sungleams kissed.

He learns that all who would be truly great
   Mix with the battling world, nor shirk their part,
But take such trials as are given by Fate
   And set them to sweet music by their art.

He only is a poet who can find
   In sorrow, happiness, in darkness, light,
Love everywhere, and lead his fellow kind
   By flowery paths towards life's sunny height.

GOLD TRESSES.

My love is now a woman grown.
   About her shoulders fall no more
Her locks, in beauty all their own.
   Their days of liberty are o'er.

No longer may, with soft caress,
   The zephyr's unseen hand uplift
Each net-like, golden-threaded tress
   To catch the sunlight's moted drift.

I know each tress, and have a name
   Whereby my memory holds it dear,
From that which is her forehead's frame
   To that which hides her shelly ear.

And one there is I loved to touch,
   On which my heart first suffered wreck,
That sometimes fell aside too much
   And showed the ivory of her neck.

And though 'tis bound upon her head
   And all its beauty hid from me,
Still other charms I see instead,
   And still am in captivity.

I see the grace of neck and ear
   Unveiled, that erst beneath the tress
But peeped, as pearly sea shells peer
   Through ocean's weedy wilderness.

Ye captive tresses that disdained
   My love, and wantoned in the wind,
I know your grief, for I was chained
   Her slave ere ye were thus confined.

She hath but gloried in our love,
   And laughs to find us strain our gyves.
Come, let us slaves unite and prove
   That power to break her bond survives.

Aid me with love her heart to chain,
   And soon, when she and I are wed,
My hands shall set ye free again
   To wanton sweetly round her head.

EN ROUTE.

By town and hamlet, field and wood,
  Past glimpses of empurpled hills,
O'er many a broad, sun-smitten flood
  And many a myriad tinkling rills,
The train swings on and brings us twain
  Each minute nearer by a mile,
While I to chafe at time am fain,
  Which holds me sundered from thy smile.

I see among the emerald trees
  Embowered, the village church spires gleam ;
I see white homestead front the breeze,
  And of our own sweet home I dream ;
While still the fleet train brings us twain
  Each minute nearer by a mile,
And fewer moments yet remain
  To hold me sundered from thy smile.

The wheat fields shimmer in the sun,
  Sleek cattle in the meadows browse,
Nor lift their heads, as past we run,
  The lithe-limbed steeds and patient cows..

And still the fleet train brings us twain
　Each minute nearer by a mile,
Till scarce a moment doth remain
　To hold me sundered from thy smile.

Onward we sweep, yet all our speed
　Leaves not pursuing night behind;
Stars sparkle in the sky's broad mead,
　And homeward plods the weary hind ;
And still the fleet train brings us twain
　Each minute nearer by a mile,
Until my heart is home again
　And I am basking in thy smile.

AT DAWN.

At dawn of day a shaft of light
Pierces the sable breast of night,
  Which, dropping many a sable plume,
  Flits far into the nether gloom,
      All silently.

At dawn of day the sun's first beam
Dispels the mist that hides the stream,
  And scatters from the hill and wood
  The clouds that there did sit and brood,
      Formless and grey.

And when the night from earth is driven,
And clouds and mist have fled from heaven,
  The waking birds take eager flight
  Up through the golden rain of light,
      With happy song.

Into my life, that knew no day,
A maiden winged a kindly ray,
  And, flying wearily and slow,
  Far fled the sombre bird of woe
      I harbored long.

My heart no longer pined in night,
The mists that hid hope's stream took flight,
  Life's hills a sunnier aspect took,
  And I found many a pleasant nook
    Within life's grove.

And now my thoughts, like birds, arise,
Singing, towards the golden skies,
  Afar from earthly doubt and strife,
  Through the pure radiance of her life,
    On wings of love.

MY STAR.

There is a star in the pure ether high,
    My other home it is,
Whereto, when sorrow threatens me, I fly,
And in my flight towards the vaulted sky
  The hated sorrows roll
  Down from my fleet-winged soul,
As from the sea gull's circling form the spray
Drops to the storm-vext bay
    Its pinions erst did kiss.

Well said the Seer, that overstudy brought
    A weariness of the flesh;
And oft my brain, worn with its overthought,
Watches the night steal past, while sleep comes not.
  Then doth my star arise
  Slowly before my eyes,
Steady, serene and cold, yet heavenly bright,
And, while my grief takes flight,
    Binds all my thoughts in leash.

No longer fear and discontent combine
    To make my future drear,
For I arise and from that star of mine
Look down and see our small earth dimly shine;

And all life's joy and pain
Their proper worth obtain,
And I to smile at all past fears begin,
For earth's discordant din
Is stilled, and God I hear.

TO A PICTURE.

O stately head, O rippling grace
   Of tresses flowing free,
O dark-eyed, queenly, thoughtful face,
   Awake and comfort me.

Since love can thrill with noble zeal
   The meanest of us all,
It may thy glorious form reveal,
   Thy tender soul recall.

Then come thou from thy gilded cage
   And nestle by my side,
And I will be thy faithful page,
   If thou wilt be my bride.

Come, trustful eyes, and trust in me,
   O sweet one, heed my cry;
Speak sad, sweet mouth, I wait for thee
   To bid me live or die.

Tell me no artist's god-like mind
   To thy fair face gave birth,
But that his vision I may find
   Alive upon this earth.

And I will seek her far and wide,
  In palace and in cot,
And love shall once more conquer pride,
  And she shall share my lot.

THE POET AND HIS RHYMES.

Whoever reads a poet's rhyme
   To find the poet there,
Might equally essay to climb
   To castles in the air.

He lives not in reality,
   Or rather, lives too much.
He makes a forest of a tree,
   A palace of a hutch.

To-day a transient pang appears
   His life's eternal sorrow,
But he is laughing through his tears
   And full of joy to-morrow.

For if there's oft a germ of truth,
   The flower is fancy's own.
'Tis the world's heart he shows, in sooth,
   And his is still unknown.

And sometimes in his happiest days,
   Without excuse or cause,
He pens the mournfullest of lays,
   To win the world's applause.

And from the saddest heart, at times,
   The merriest stanzas flow.
Friend, think not by the poet's rhymes
   The poet's heart to know.

TO AN INFANT.

O little one, new born,
  I would I were like thee ;
Then were this whole world's scorn
  And praise alike to me.

Then would I look on life
  As do thine azure eyes,
And know how vain its strife,
  How paltry what we prize.

Tradition cannot claim
  Dominion over thee,
Nor fear the pinions maim
  Of thy young soul and free.

All things to thee are new.
  Thy mind runs in no groove.
Thou dost both false and true
  Question alike, and prove.

Thou art no shadowy soul,
  But the incarnate " I ",
And thou wilt reach thy goal,
  Or failing, thou wouldst die.

Indomitable will
    That makes us all obey,—
If I were childlike still,
    I were more man to-day.

TO SCOTLAND.

Miles upon miles of ocean
  'Twixt Scotland roll and me.
Its hills and dales I have not seen,
  And scarce expect to see.
The homestead of my fathers
  The keen ploughshare has torn,
And where the hearth once welcomed all
  Waves now the golden corn.

Oh, Canada, my country,
  My love for thee is deep,
Yet I fain would see the old church-yard
  Where my forefathers sleep.
And fondly, ever fondly,
  My heart in secret yearns,
That its songs may find a welcome
  In the bonnie land of Burns.

Upon the Scottish heather
  I opened not my eyes,
I cannot speak the sweet Scotch tongue,
  Remote my pathway lies ;
Yet Scotland, mother Scotland,
  Though fate us twain may part,
I claim my heritage of thee,
  For I have the Scottish heart.

ROSINA VOKES.

The years may come, the years may go,
    And many a song be sung
Across the footlight's golden glow
    By many a silvery tongue,
But though new divas charm the ear,
    Still memory shall recall
One song we nevermore shall hear:
    " His 'art was true to Poll."

For who that hath the singer's heart
    Will care to sing that song
To those whom She, with witching art,
    Had held in thrall so long ?
Let other songs our pulses stir,
    Delight us with them all,
But leave unsung for sake of her
    " His 'art was true to Poll."

Time was when every heart beat high,
    Each lip was wreathed in smiles
To hear her sing that melody
    With all her witching wiles ;
But now, 'twould be no song of mirth,
    'Twould bid the sad tears fall,
For though She dwells no more on earth,
    Our 'arts are true to Poll.

A LITTLE MAID.

I know a maid beyond compare
For virtue sweet and beauty rare.
Her eyes are turquoise and her hair
    Is sunlight netted.

She has her lovers, great and small,
The quiet student, wise and tall,
The child that hugs its battered doll,—
    By them she's petted.

Her heart seems ever warm and gay,
In smiles and kindly words, each day,
She scatters round her on life's way
    Love beyond measure.

The wild flowers, as she passes by,
Bloom sweeter for her being nigh ;
The bird that mounts into the sky
    Sings for her pleasure.

Her sorrows she is wont to hide,
Her joys she shares on every side ;
She is her doting mother's pride,
    Her father's jewel.

If we, who style this world so bad,
But strove, like her, to make it glad,
Life then would seem by far less sad,
    Nor half so cruel.

SAMSON AND DELILAH.

Thou art o'erbold, Delilah, thus to try
 Thy traitorous arts upon a soul like mine,
And lure me to eternal slavery
 With glances warm like wine.

One clasp of my strong hands at will could break
 Thy tender body, like a fragile flower.
How darest thou prey of my heart to make,
 And plot against my power?

Hast thou no fear the brute in me will rise,
 Wrathful, and tear thy shapely limbs apart,
And dull the jewelled lustre of thine eyes,
 And still thy faithless heart?

Why dost thou let me look upon thy face,
 And see myself embowered in thine eyes,
And every curve of thy lithe figure trace
 Beneath thy robe's disguise.

What harm have I wrought thee that thou
  shouldst stand
 And menace all my life with one great woe?
Thou hast me in the hollow of thy hand—
 Take me or let me go!

MY LADY'S BONNET.

My lady has a stylish bonnet,
　Bedecked with ribands, gay and bright,
And with a song bird perched upon it,
　With tiny wings outspread for flight.

Its little beak is opened wide,
　As though in its most joyous trill
The harmless thing had suddenly died.
　One waits to hear it carol still.

My lady has a tender heart,
　She feeds the poor, instructs the young,
At tale of woe her tears will start,
　And words of kindness throng her tongue.

My lady's eyes are full of glee,
　But cloud and with just anger flash
If in her walk she chance to see
　Some poor beast cringe beneath the lash.

My lady has a stylish bonnet,
　Bedecked with ribands gay and bright,
But with a slaughtered bird upon it.—
　My gentle lady, is this right?

FLOWERS AND FEARS.

She had been in the fields at play
   Through golden summer hours,
And brought with her, at close of day,
   A cluster of wild flowers.

And when she slept, we went to see
   The little one at rest,
Our own sweet flower, and there, ah, me!
   The flowers lay on her breast.

Her little brow was smooth and white,
   Her merry eyes were closed,
She smiled, as though some heavenly sprite
   Whispered as she reposed.

She looked so pure, so white, so fair
   Below the ominous flowers,
She seemed a blossom plucked from care
   To bloom in heavenly bowers.

And oh, the whelming flood of pain,
   The sudden sense of dearth!
We kissed her o'er and o'er again,
   And brought her back to earth.

THE ROSEBUD.

In my garden a rosebud is growing, is growing,
    So fast, 'twill be blossoming soon.
Around it the zephyrs are balmily blowing,
    The sweet scented zephyrs of June,
            Of June,
    The odorous zephyrs of June.

My love shall watch o'er, and protect, and protect it,
    While shyly its petals unfold.
The bees shall not rob nor the canker affect it,
    Nor night make it tremble with cold,
            With cold,
    Nor night make it shudder with cold.

And when it is blown, I'll bear it, I'll bear it
    To her whom I worship alone.
On her beauteous bosom she'll lay it and wear it
    And rival its charms by her own,
            Her own,
    And shame all its grace by her own.

NIL DESPERANDUM.

Life with life is woven in.
  Neither sorrow nor delight,
Neither nobleness nor sin,
      Known to one
      But falls upon
  All men with its grace or blight.

He who sinks into despair,
  He who from his task recoils,
Makes his fellow-laborers bear
      On life's road
      A heavier load.
  Some one for each sluggard toils.

What though failure crown our task!
  'Tis the portal to success.
Often Fortune wears a mask.
      Face the strife
      And live your life;
  Be no coward in distress!

FLESH AND SPIRIT.

Say what you will,
If love would have its fill,
   Though it may feed long on the one dear face,
   It never is content, save in embrace.

Say what you will,
Though passion have its fill,
   It never is content, nor has delight,
   If love come not to sanctify the rite.

Harmonious flesh and spirit,
These only shall inherit
   The joys of earth, and in the dread To Be
   Not death itself shall break that unity.

Woe to the narrow heart
Would strive these twain to part ;
   Look down the ages, through the world's mad din,
   This is the one unpardonable sin.

IN CHURCH.

I never feel so near to God and heaven
  As when I kneel in worship at thy side,
And hear thy humble prayer to be forgiven
  For sake of Him who for our saving died.

And though I do not mingle with thy prayer
  Plea of my own, but, silent, bow my head,
So close our souls are knit, I seem to share
  The bounteous blessings God on thee doth shed.

I hear the choir their joyous praises singing,
  But not their voices soften my flint heart:
Thine only in my inmost soul is ringing,
  Bidding peace enter, grief and sin depart.

And as the music through my pulse is stealing,
  The rampart of my pride a ruin falls,
Even as of old the Jewish trumpets' pealing
  Shook down of haughty Jericho the walls.

SUCCOR THE CHILDREN.

Wan hands that never grasped a flower,
    Ears stranger to the wild bird's song,
To rule, where shall they find the power?
    How wage life's battle, right the wrong?

When the great hour of duty comes,
.   How shall they meet the mighty toil,
Whose blood is tainted by the slums,
    Whose ears know but the street's turmoil?

Succor the children of the street,
    And teach them in the fields to play,
Nor let them in the stifling heat
    Of crowded cities fade away;

That, when we drop the thread of life
    And, dreamless, sleep beneath the sod,
They may be ready for the strife
    That brings this planet nearer God.

THE SUNSET LESSON.

I watched the sun one summer eve
  Sink slowly in the west,
And the quiet sea and fleecy clouds
  In rosy robes were dressed.

I saw the evening glide away,
  Yet still the sea and sky,
As faint the star-zoned twilight grew,
  Were full of majesty.

And as, upon the breezy hill,
  I turned to sky and sea,
Methought that nature spake and bade
  My spirit guileless be,

That, as the deepening shades of age
  Close round me, like the night,
The memory of my past might still
  Life's evening gild with light.

AS FROM THE NECTAR-LADEN LILY.

As from the nectar-laden
  Lily the wild bee sips,
A British queen, sweet maiden,
  Drained with her loving lips
The poison that was filling
  Her husband's veins with death, ·
Her love with new life thrilling
  His heart with each drawn breath.

Not less thy love, sweet maiden,
  Nor less thy bravery,
For when I came, o'erladen
  With poisoned hopes, to thee,
With smiles and shy caresses
  The venom thou didst drain,
And, healing my distresses,
  Didst give new life again.

MUMMY THOUGHTS.

Once those who sought for relics of the past
   Stumbled by chance on an Etrurian tomb,
   And saw a monarch sitting in the gloom,
Sceptred and crowned.   Their eager hearts beat fast,
And on the masonry themselves they cast,
   To seize the wonder.   As, throughout the room,
   The axe stroke rang, it knelled the monarch's doom.
He fell to dust, and left them all aghast.

So, oft while searching through the realms of mind,
   I have discovered many a kingly thought,
   In solitary grandeur throned and crowned,
And striven to bear it forth, only to find
   That, when the first stroke of my pen did sound,
   It fell to dust, and lo! I had it not.

TO CERTAIN NATURE POETS.

Friends,—such I call ye, for it is not meet
  To hail ye brethren in the tuneful art,
  Since I but falter, though of earnest heart,—
Friends, I have thought, reading your measures sweet,
Your verses, though with many a charm replete,
  Were bettered did they some high thought impart,
  Or in man's conscience plant a sudden dart.
Why proffer roses when the world craves wheat?

Who paints a picture hath ill done his task,
  If he show not the soul in that he paints.
  Why give to mere description all your lays
While what the eye beholds is but a mask
  To some grand truth the poet's hand should raise,
  Revealing that for which man's spirit faints.

THE PATRIARCH'S DEATH.

The birds that twitter in the budding trees
 And build their nests in some umbrageous grove,
 Through early summer guard the young they love,
And fill the air with tuneful melodies.
Then, as the fledgelings wake from dreamful ease,
 Eager throughout the unknown world to rove,
 The parents teach them their new strength to prove,
And beat with fearless wings the summer breeze.

And then the nest sways empty on the bough.
 The parents, weary, although sweet the task,
  Take flight to other haunts, to rest from care.
 The fledgelings in the glowing sunbeams bask,
  Living their life.   So is it everywhere,—
The patriarch dies; he is but resting now.

OH, WERE IT NOT.

Oh, were it not for one fair face,
　One angel voice, one loving smile,
The world would be a dreary place,
　And life to me not worth the while.

Methinks the sun shines but to show
　How wondrous fair the maiden is ;
Methinks the warm winds only blow
　That they may kiss her draperies.

I know the roses bloom that they
　May live an hour upon her breast ;
I know that I would willingly
　Share their brief life to share their nest.

FAREWELL.

When the heart speaks, the lips are still,
  And if I cannot say farewell,
'Tis that a thousand yearnings thrill
  My heart, and hold my lips in spell.

Let thine own heart the thoughts express
  My lips would speak.   Yet why repine ?
I knew thee, and, at least, can bless
  Thy life, though sundered far from mine.

THE TIDE.

Twice in the day a mighty tide there rolls
  Throughout our city streets,
A limitless, deep sea of human souls,
  Each wave, a heart that beats.

Ah, me! what various ships are drifting there,
  Upon that living sea;
What guile and innocence, what joy, what care,
  What utter misery!

At morn it ebbs far from home's golden shore
  Into the sea of life,
Where its dark billows meet and foam and roar
  In never-ending strife.

At night it flows, far from the mart's turmoil,
  Backward upon its way,
Where wives and children bring sweet rest from toil,
  Till dawns another day.

From year to year 'tis thus these waters move,
  Life's duties to fulfill;
Obedient to the silvery moon of love,
  That rules them at its will.

MY COMRADE.

Could I have had you made a boy,
  And both be young through life,
Methinks I might forgo the joy
  Of calling you my wife.

For sweet as is the kiss of love
  And all our converse staid,
Still dearer to our hearts doth prove
  Some wayward escapade.

When from behind your glistening foil
  You dare me to the fray,
From sober spousehood I recoil ;
  It is " en garde " straightway.

And when we urge our light canoe
  Upon some sparkling tide,
More prone am I to think of you
  As comrade than as bride.

Ah, were you but a youth, like me,
  Who could, unawed, recline
By huge camp fire, beneath some tree,
  Upon a couch of pine ;

And could you press through marsh and brake
  And thrive on hunter's food,
What sweet excursions we might make
  To nature's solitude !

Yet if you were a youth, some maid
  Might lure you from my side,
So I shall wish you still, comrade,
  My dainty, fair-haired bride.

MY GIFT.

I bring a gift that all may bring,
　　So common 'tis to human kind ;
And yet it is so rare, a king
　　His crown for it had well resigned.

It is a gift gold cannot buy,
　　And one which never can be sold ;
A gift no mortal can deny,
　　And one that fades not, nor grows old.

And while I would not have it spurned,
　　Such is my heart's perversity,
Unless I know my gift returned,
　　Life hath no joy in store for me.

HAMLIN'S MILL.

Brightly the sun that summer day
  Upon the charming scene was shining,
And warm the thrifty village lay,
  Amid its silent fields reclining.
The river, like a silver thread,
  Wound round the hazy, shimmering hill,
Till, plunging o'er the dam, it fled
  In eddies down to Hamlin's Mill.

Along the pathway, through the grove,
  Beneath the shady trees, we hurried.
The birds were twittering above,
  While in and out the squirrels scurried.
We took the narrow road which wound,
  Through clearings that were smoking still ;
And soon our merry chat was drowned
  Amidst the noise at Hamlin's Mill.

We stood within the sunlit room
  And watched the busy bobbins turning ;
Then gathered round a jangling loom,
  The flying shuttle's secret learning.
Across the mossy flume we crept,
  Whose leaky sides their burden spill,
And stood beside the pond, where slept
  The giant power of Hamlin's Mill.

Beside the ceaseless loom of fate
  We stand and watch what it is weaving.
The warp is spun of love and hate,
  The woof of merriment and grieving.
But far beyond earth's noise and dust,
  There rules the one stupendous Will,
The power in which His creatures trust,
  As in the mill-pond Hamlin's Mill.

A BALLADE OF JOY.

Dear one, who wast chosen, ere time was made,
　The heart of my heart and my wife to be ;
Who cam'st, with the gifts of the gods arrayed,
　To lighten the labors of life for me ;
　Ere yet I had looked on the face of thee,
My soul dreamed dreams and awoke and said :
　" None other is worthier love than she,
And earth shall be heaven when we are wed."

But woe as a burden on man is laid,
　And the soul finds its vision not readily.
Between us came many a mocking shade,
　That smiled with the smile of my fantasy,
　And I thought, can it be I have met with thee ?
Then the arrows of truth through the false were sped,
　And I heard thy soul murmuring cheeringly,
" The earth shall be heaven when we are wed."

Like streams in the hollows of hills that played,
　Though sundered by league upon league they be,
That, slipping through tangles of sun and shade,
　Meet, mingle and flow to the shoreless sea,
　At last my soul met with the soul of thee,
　And woes fell from me as leaves fall dead
When winds have wakened the sleeping tree,
And earth became heaven when we were wed.

ENVOI.

And now, though years like the birds may flee,
  And death draw nigh us with noiseless tread,
I reek not how soon may the summons be,
  For earth became heaven when we were wed.

REMEMBRANCE.

(From the German of Fredrich Matthison.)

I think of thee
When through the brake
The nightingales sweet music make.
　When dost thou think of me ?

I think of thee
By the shady well,
Under the twilight's glimmering spell.
　Where dost thou think of me ?

I think of thee
With pleasant pain,
.With yearning, while the hot tears rain.
　How dost thou think of me ?

Oh, think of me
Till in some star
We meet again.　However far,
　I think of none but thee.

THE GLOVE.

A narrow glen with winding sides,
　　Bestrewn with rocks and gloomed with trees,
　　Grey, rolling clouds, chased by the breeze,
A stream, which through the valley glides.

Among the trees that climb the hill
　　The eager squirrels scold the crows,
　　And sharply sound the sudden blows
Of some woodpecker's greedy bill.

The blood root, crouching in the grass,
　　From its protecting broad leaf peers ;
　　The horse tails shake aloft their spears,
Like foemen, at us as we pass.

Here wandering with a friend I love,
　　Our speech with sparrow-chatter drowned,
　　He in the little valley found
An early violet, I a glove.

The flower grew beside a stone,
　　And shyly peered above the sod,
　　While, distant from it not a rod,
The dainty glove lay all alone.

Some child had drawn it from her hand
  To dabble in the sunny spring,
  And then, the thoughtless little thing,
Had left it lying on the rand.

And as I saw the symbols there
  Of budding life and blossoming spring,
  Arose and from my heart took wing
To heaven a brief and heartfelt prayer :

O little child, whoe'er thou art,
  And in whatever station set,
  Be modest, like the violet,
And act in life an earnest part,

That, as the streamlet by the sun
  Is gently lifted to the skies,
  Thy soul may unto heaven arise
Whene'er its earthly course is run.

THE MAGIC BOW.

(From the French of Charles Cros.)

Rippling low to her dainty feet,
Tress with tress did mingle and meet,
Yellow as ripening August wheat.

Her voice had an eerie melody,
Like that of an angel or a fay.
Beneath dusk lashes her eyes shone gray.

He by no rival swain set store,
As valleys through, or mountains o'er,
The maid upon his steed he bore.

For all the land had held not one
That she in her pride would look upon
To the day she met him, and was undone.

Love did her fond heart so enchain
That when her lover smiled disdain,
She to sicken and die was fain.

As she lay dying on his arm,
She said, " Bind thy bow with my locks, to charm
The maid to whom thy heart grows warm."

One long, wild kiss, and the maid was dead.
The shimmering aureole round her head
He bound to his bow, as she had said

Then as a blind man mournfully
Sweeps his Cremona, so did he,
And went forth, seeking charity.

And all were thrilled with ecstasy,
For the dead lived within the lay,
And with her songs all hearts did sway.

The king showered honors on his head ;
The dark-eyed queen, to honor dead,
With him by moonlight swiftly fled.

But when, to please her, he essayed
To play, no more the bow obeyed,
But mournfully did him upbraid.

And at its plaint the sinful twain
In mid-flight by remorse were slain,
And the dead had her pledge again.

Her locks that to her dainty feet
Rippling low, did mingle and meet,
Yellow as ripening August wheat.

AT THE SEASIDE.

O sun, with thy ardent glance,
　Thou hast made my darling flush !
But the swarthier tints enhance
　The charms of her modest blush.
Thou hast lent thy warmth and light
　To the gleam of her melting eyes,
Till a glance in their depths so bright
　Seems a peep into Paradise.

O sea, with thy great white arms,
　Thou hast stolen my love from me !
Thou hast clasped to thy breast her charms ;
　She has rested her head on thee.
Thou hast tangled her silken hair,
　And kissed her face and her lips—
Ah ! Love, he is false !　Beware
　Of that spoiler of men and ships !

THE ORPHANS.

Shall walls have pity and man's heart have none ?
   Shall walls protect and man refuse to aid ?
   At Christmas, when our children are arrayed
In furs, shall orphans crouch behind a stone
To hide them from the storm ?   Is there not one
   Will see the outstretched hand of that frail maid,
   To whom the baby brother clings, afraid ?
Will no ear heed when hunger makes its moan ?

No father's arm about their forms is thrown
   To shield them from distress, no mother's love
   Draws them within the shelter of her breast.
Those tender souls must front the world alone ;
   But, if Christ came not vainly from above,
   Some noble heart will aid them, thus distressed.

ALADDIN'S LAMP.

Aladdin's lamp of Eastern tale,
  Which claimed my simple faith in youth,
Its loss no longer I bewail,
  But hold it mine in very truth.

The geni waits but my command
  To raise me, and, as swift as thought,
Bear me abroad, from land to land,
  Wherever I would fain be brought.

Amid the silent northern snows,
  Or where Egyptian deserts burn,
Wherever man has been, he goes,
  And tells me all I wish to learn.

He tells me how the stars had birth,
  And how their wondrous cycles run,
Or places me beyond the earth,
  Unharmed, upon the giant sun.

Through him I learn what Science knows,
  How this vast universe began ;
How life, from mean beginnings, rose
  High as God's noblest creature, man.

On me dawns many a truth profound
   About the swinging earth I tread,
That it is one vast burying ground,
   The living living through the dead,

That where once flowed the ocean's tide,
   Now stand the homes of countless souls ;
That where once mountains rose in pride,
   Billow on foaming billow rolls.

The geni stems the flood of time,
   And bears me almost to its source ;
Then as we float, bids scenes sublime
   And sad and happy shore our course.

I see the tower of Babel rise,
   With busy builders everywhere,
Up, ever up, towards the skies,
   Spearing the azure depths of air.

I hear a voice from out a cloud,
   And see the workmen making signs,—
How humble God can make the proud !
   How easily mar man's best designs !

I see the wild Light Tresses fall ·
   In cruel waves on fated Rome,
And in an emperor's audience hall
   I see the jackals make their home.

Sleek monks I see within their cells,
  And knights in burnished armor housed.
I hear the chime of marriage bells
  For maids whom death hath long espoused.

I hear the poet's stirring strain,
  That wins him immortality,
And weep with such as found with pain
  Their idol but ignoble clay.

Writ by the fearless Luther pen,
  The words that stirred the world I see ;
I hear the tramp of arméd men,
  And know that thought, at last, is free.

The joys and hopes, the griefs and fears,
  Defeats and conquests of the race,
Through all the swift, eventful years,
  The geni at my wish will trace.

And though he builds no palace vast
  For me, nor gives me queen for bride,
While I am free to all the past,
  I ask from him no boon beside.

SONG.

When a maiden's heart is tender,
  And her soul as pure as snow ;
When her eyes, with sunny splendor,.
  Set her countenance aglow ;
When her every move discovers
  Newer graces without end,
She can win a hundred lovers,—
  Yet may hunger for a friend.

Pearly teeth and curly tresses,
  Ruby lips, in smiles that part,
These will lure a man's caresses,
  Easily enslave his heart ;
Yet, when all is said and over,
  Even though souls in passion blend,
She has only one more lover,
  And may hunger for a friend.

Blind I am not, no, nor callous ;
  Beauty hath its charm for me.
Yet would I, beyond life's shallows,
  Push towards the depthless sea.
Friendship's true, and Love's a rover,
  Love is selfish in the end.
Choose thee, Sweet, whatever lover,
  Let me still remain thy friend.

QUATRAINS.

I.

The oyster turns into a gem
    The sand that chafes it long ;
My woes, can I not banish them,
    I round into a song.

II.

Fear less the villain than the fool.
    The villain may be read,
But heaven itself can set no rule
    To judge an addled head.

III.

Nurse thou no sorrow, only learn
    All that it has to teach,
And lo, a glorious gem shall burn
    Upon the brow of each.

IV.

The bard alone immortal is ;
    In death he liveth still,
And, godlike, with a word of his
    Makes deathless whom he will.

V.

Would they but speak who proved but weak
　　To those who think self strong,
How they would cry, continually,
　　" Beware the first small wrong ! "

VI.

To Felix Morris.

Twin arts are ours, to act and write,
　　And yours, perhaps, the greater is ;
You bring the world before men's sight,
　　I can but proffer fantasies.

VII.

Flowers are earth's resurrection, yet the rocks,
　　Ere raised in blossoms, first shall fall to dust.
Take comfort, then, O brother, when life mocks
　　Thine aspirations, as perforce life must.

VIII.

Man loves the ideal and not the maid ;
　　Her he but garlands with hopes and dreams,
And worships, not her in those wreaths arrayed,
　　But the vision of fancy that then she seems.

www.ingramcontent.com/pod-product-compliance
Lightning Source LLC
Chambersburg PA
CBHW021131020726
47500CB00003B/1032